# COordination IS THE KEY to a HAPPY LIFE

## TALES THREE

BY
STACEY ANDRADE

DESIGN AND ILLUSTRATION
BY DIANE O'CONNOR

Published by teaseaproductions,
Pinole, CA,  April 1, 2024

ISBN 979-8-218-38451-7

Printed in the United States of America

# DEDICATION

THIS BOOK IS DEDICATED TO MY MUCH, MUCH, OLDER SISTERS, GILDA AND KAREN. I CAME INTO THIS WORLD WITH TWO INSTANT BEST FRIENDS. MY SISTERS HAVE BEEN MY SUPPORT SYSTEM AND MY CHAMPIONS THROUGHOUT MY ENTIRE JOURNEY. MY SISTERS HAVE BROUGHT SO MUCH JOY AND LAUGHTER TO MY LIFE. GILDA AND KAREN TOOK OUR DAD INTO THEIR HOMES WHEN HE NEEDED HELP, AND FOR THIS I WILL FOREVER BE IN THEIR DEBT. I JUST WISH THEIR FEET WEREN'T SO BIG - I COULD'VE BEEN BORROWING THEIR SHOES ALL THESE YEARS.

# ACKNOWLEDGEMENTS

I WOULD LIKE TO THANK MY HUSBAND, DEREK, FOR HIS UNWAVERING SUPPORT THROUGH ALL MY CREATIVE ENDEAVORS. I COULD NOT HAVE PURSUED MY DREAMS WITHOUT YOUR LOVE AND SUPPORT.

THANK YOU TO ALL MY AMAZING FRIENDS AND FAMILY FOR THEIR SUPPORT.

# Table Of Contents

---

# What's a Mudbug

In the dead of winter, my husband Kyle, sat in his favorite chair, plucking on his bass guitar.

"Alice, guess what?"

"That sounds ominous. What?"

"Red Dirt Band got the gig at the Isleton Crawdad Festival. Two days, three stages, and great money."

"Awesome, dude. What the hell is a crawdad?"

"You don't know what a crawdad is? It's a mudbug."

"Cool, what the hell is a mudbug? Do you eat it?"

"Sure do. They're like little lobsters with ten legs. You pull the heads off and suck out the meat. You really need a platter of mudbugs. There's not much meat in mudbugs."

"Ya, I think I'll skip this gig. Thanks anyway."

"No, you can't. I need you to roadie."

"What? Kyle, I'm five-foot-two. Can't you find a bigger roadie?"

"Don't worry, my bro Rick, is coming to help, too."

The Crawdad Festival was over Father's Day weekend. Not only did I have to deal with a weekend with mudbugs, but I was also missing Father's Day with my dad. Red Dirt Band better pay me well.

The heat wave was in full gear. The news said temperatures would be well over a hundred all weekend. I hoped there would be covers over the stages for our fair-skinned band.

Red Dirt Band consisted of Kyle on bass and vocals; Kyle's brother, Will, lead singer and guitarist; and a drummer. Red Dirt has a lot of original songs. Not just anyone can drum for them. Red Dirt had lost their drummer, so a musician friend recommended his friend, Jim.

Kyle, Will, and I met Rick, at a gas station halfway to Isleton.

"Hey Rick, ready to party?" Kyle asked.

"Sure, this is going to be great. I love Cajun music."

"Cool, follow us. They'll have parking for the bands."

Jim, the drummer, had planned to meet us at the first stage they'd be playing at.

It was also our wedding anniversary. I had never been to Isleton. Kyle had reserved a nice room for us at the Ryde Hotel. The Ryde Hotel was about two miles down the river from Isleton. Ryde was a cool art deco hotel that sat on the Delta River.

We pulled into the town of Isleton. Vendors were busy setting up their booths. The festival ran the length of Main Street. Kyle pulled up to a sign that said, "Band Parking."

"Hey, you can't park here." A man with an official-looking vest on barked at us.

"Hey man, I'm with the Red Dirt Band. We're playing this stage next. Can we park here and unload?"

"No, man, you can't park here. There's not enough room. Go to the field behind Isleton. A golf cart will pick up your instruments."

My husband is very detail-oriented. I knew his butt cheeks were tightening, and he would be grinding his teeth.

"Don't worry, Kyle. The golf cart will pick us up, and you'll start on time." I said as I rubbed his back.

"They're not taking my Steinberger Bass. It's not replaceable. I'll just walk it in."

We pulled into the field behind Main Street. Red Dirt's first gig of the day wasn't for an hour. The trek back to the stage at least half of a mile. The festival seemed chaotic and unorganized. You never really know what you're walking into when you book a gig.

Kyle, Rick, and I stood by the truck waiting for the golf cart that never appeared. Time was ticking away.

"You and Rick head to the stage. Hopefully, Jim is setting up his drums. I'll wait here and try to chase down one of the golf carts and bring your gear to the stage as soon as possible."

Kyle's face scrunched up. He grabbed his bass. Kyle and Rick took off for town.

I spent the next twenty minutes chasing down golf carts in the dusty field. I saw an empty one and chased the golf cart driver until he stopped. I explained my predicament, and he helped me load the small golf cart with instruments and mics. I was already tired, and we still had three gigs on three different stages that day.

By some miracle, we got Red Dirt on stage that day with two minutes to spare. The band sounded great. I couldn't really enjoy them because I was freaked out about getting the band and instruments to the next stage in this crowd. Everyone I talked to kept giving me the name of the guy in charge, but I had yet to find this mysterious guy.

Rick and I were trying to figure out the logistics.

"Rick, I'm going to go and see where the next stage is and find out if they have parking there."

"Good luck, this is a real shit show. It's hot as hell. Keep drinking water."

As the day went on, we all realized there was no parking for the bands at any of the stages. Getting the talent and their instruments to the next stage became a nightmare. Rick and I were running and pushing our way through the crowds of drunk bikers and festival goers with equipment piled in our hands.

At the second gig of the day, I came running to the stage with mics and mic stands in my hand, and Kyle said, "Where have you been, Alice? A friend of mine saw you in town and said you had a cop against the wall screaming at him about not having parking for the twenty bands. I figured they arrested you."

"It's still early, Kyle. Don't count your earnings just yet. You still might have to bail me out of jail tonight."

"I know, sweetie, you and Rick are saving the day. There's no way we could've done this without you guys," said Kyle.

"Sweetie, we can't leave the instruments. Could you go get us a twelve-pack of beer?"

"Sure, Kyle, you know, this might be the best anniversary ever."

With a sheepish grin, Kyle handed me a twenty, and off I went into the drunk crowd. Kyle's lucky he's cute; otherwise, he would be buried in the backyard.

Red Dirt's second gig would start in ten minutes. When I left, the drummer was bouncing off the walls. I think some artificial energy might be in play. This gig was going south fast.

I pushed my way through the drunk bikers until I saw a sign that said General Store. I ran to the back of the store. The whole store looked like a hurricane hit it. I saw one pack of Budweiser left. I jumped on it like it was a fumbled ball.

As I left the store, I noticed the crowd was thicker and drunker. I had on shorts and a cute little top.

Man, I should've asked Rick to come with me. I put the twelve-pack on my head and used my old waitressing skills to push through the crowd. A biker who was as big as my kitchen pointed to me with my twelve-pack on my head and screamed, "Look, it's the woman of my dreams."

The crowd roared, and I ran like hell,

trying to keep the twelve-pack from slipping off my head.

The last stage of the day had no cover over it. The temperatures were rising, and you could see drunk festivalgoers dropping like flies. Kyle and Will were screaming for sunscreen. I threw my sunscreen to Kyle. He lathered up and tossed it to Will. The band started to play.

The audience huddled under the one shade tree by the stage. Sweat was dripping off the band's faces. I worried they'd get heat stroke. Looking at the band, I could tell something was wrong.

"Alice, I can't see. The sunscreen got in my eyes." I could tell Will was having the same problem. Great, now I have a blind band. I emptied my water bottle on a rag I found in the band's gear and threw it up to Kyle. I looked at Rick, and we both shook our heads.

Rick and I had spent the whole day fighting people for parking spaces and hunting down the elusive golf carts. Running from one end of town to the other with the band's equipment in the heat.

Turns out Jim, the drummer for the day, should've been at an A.A. meeting or a rehabilitation center. Jim was a loose cannon. I hoped he could maintain until the gigs were over. Running in the heat gave me my first case of heat stroke. My head pounded.

"Alice, I'm so sorry our anniversary didn't turn out like we wanted."

"Ya think?" I screamed.

"Let's go back to the beautiful hotel and have a nice dinner and lots of aspirin." I slammed three aspirins and headed to the car in the field.

Kyle and I checked into the gorgeous hotel. The hotel staff took our bags up to our room while we sat on the deck outside the bar. Kyle ordered a bunch of tapas and drinks. Frank Sinatra rang out of the speakers. Maybe this anniversary will turn around after all.

The waitress came and gave us our drinks and appetizers. When she put the last tapas plate on our table, Jim's face peaked around the corner. My stomach dropped.

"Hey guys, have you seen Will?" Jim asked.

"No, Jim. He's still in town. What do you need?" Kyle asked.

"I'm out of money, and I was wondering if I could crash here with Will tonight. I want to be fresh for the gigs tomorrow."

I thought, dude, you haven't been fresh for decades. So, Kyle, Jim, and I enjoyed our anniversary appetizers while listening to Frank Sinatra belt out, "I Did It My Way."

"Kyle, I'm going to the room."

The room was beautiful, but I didn't see a bathroom. My head wouldn't stop pounding from the heatstroke. The aspirins were not working. My lip started to quiver.

I went to the bar. Jim and Kyle seemed to really be enjoying our anniversary. The woman who checked us in sat at the bar.

"Excuse me, we just checked in. Our room is great, but I didn't see a bathroom. Where's our bathroom?"

"It's a European room."

"I'm sorry, what?"

"Means you're a peeing down the hall."

Kyle and Jim began cracking up. I just wanted to hit someone. Twice. Perhaps Jim.

"There's a water closet down the hall from your room. There's a picture of a toilet on the door. You'll see it."

"Also, the room feels like a hot house because of the heat-wave. Where's the air-conditioner?" I asked the nice hotel worker.

"There is no air-conditioner."

I must have had quite the facial expression. The whole bar got quiet. I started to cry, and Kyle escorted me to our hothouse room.

The hotel had a wedding that day, and

the wedding guests were down one floor right below our room. The drunker the wedding guests got, the louder their voices rang out in our room. Around four in the morning, Kyle went to the window and started to mimic the loud woman's voice. We were like little kids. The guests couldn't figure out where Kyle's voice was coming from. Kyle and I laughed for the first time that day.

The hotel comped our room because we never did get to sleep with the loud wedding guests right outside our window. We checked out the next morning and headed to the day's gigs.

The second day was more of the same. At the end of the festival, we packed up and were ready to get the hell outta Dodge.

Rick came over to Kyle and whispered, "I hate to tell you this, but my truck won't start." Kyle looked defeated. We all helped move the equipment out of Rick's truck and filled Jim's van and our truck with all the equipment. Rick would stay behind and wait for the tow truck.

"Alice, Jim might've had a little too much beer today. Could you drive him and his van? Will and I will meet you in Crockett."

"Sure, Kyle. I've never driven a van, but whatever gets me out of this town."

Kyle and Will followed Jim and I as we headed out of town. I think Jim's van was the first van ever made. The steering wheel had duct tape on it, and the van smelled like garbage bags after a weeklong party.

Jim and I approached the Antioch Bridge. The bridge had to be the tallest and narrowest bridge I'd ever been on. Being afraid of heights, I began a conversation with Jim to keep my mind off the bridge.

"So, Jim, what's the deal with the duct tape on the steering wheel?"

Jim and I were at the highest point on this menacing bridge when he told me, "Ah, damn, that's just to keep the steering wheel from falling off."

I looked into the rear-view mirror and saw Kyle laughing with his brother and enjoying his pocket full of money, and I thought, if I make it over this bridge, I will end Kyle, and maybe Jim, too.

We somehow made it home in one piece. Kyle kept thanking me for all Rick, and I did to make the gig come off great.

My girlfriend, Carla, called the next day. I told her all the bloody details of the anniversary weekend. She said, "Mothers always tell you, don't date musicians. You just didn't listen."

# MOM

I jumped into my car and drove to El Cerrito Plaza to do some grocery shopping. As soon as I got home, my phone rang.

"Hello."

"Hi, it's your mom."

"I know your voice, Mom. What's going on?"

"I just saw you at the Plaza."

"You did; why didn't you say hello?"

"Because you looked crazy, Steph. Your hair was nuts, and I'm not sure what the hell you were wearing. I didn't want anyone to know I knew you."

"Wow, okay, Mom, anything else?"

"Yes, Stephanie, do me a favor and look into a mirror before you leave the house."

"You got it, Mom. Is that it?"

"While I have you, Steph, I read this article."

"Oh my God, not an article."

"Steph, I read this article that said if you eat a lot of potatoes, it can help with those dark circles under your eyes. You should get some potatoes."

"Okay, Mom. Now that I'm ready to conquer the world, I'll be going."

"Okay, Steph, have a great day."

"How can it not be, Mom? How can it not be?"

## Frida Kahlo saved my Ass

I pulled into the driveway and slammed on my brakes, just missing the garage door. Running late again. Why did I take that last call at work?

Grabbing my purse, water bottle, and backpack, with my keys somewhere under the pile stabbing my finger, I ran to the door, fumbled with the keys, unlocked it, and fell into the foyer, dropping my pile of crap.

"Laurie, aren't you ushering in the City tonight?" My husband, Danny, sat in his chair with his usual calm, collected self.

"Why, Yes, I am. Pray for good traffic heading into the City. I'm running late."

Danny laughed with a sympathetic tilt of his head. "Ahh, you're adorable. No traffic."

"It could happen. Sometimes it happens. Once it happened. Okay, it hasn't happened in this century."

As I ran through the house, tearing off my work clothes and grabbing the night's attire, I wished I had time to eat something. I tripped, trying to put my pants on in midair.

No time for dinner. Damn.

"Even if there are no wrecks, I'll be lucky to make it to the theater on time."

I made four or five trips to the car. Breathless, I threw my coat, refreshed water bottle, and phone in the trunk of the car.

Racing into the house, I grabbed the mail and threw it on the counter. I kissed my pug and Danny on the cheek. "Have a good night, you two. You'll both be snoring when I get home."

Traffic was heavy on Highway 80, which left little room for wrecks or flat tires on the bridge. My heart rate was up. My fingers gripped the steering wheel as if that would make the traffic behave.

Traffic came to a screeching halt before the toll plaza.

"Come on, what's going on?" Then, above the toll plaza, it flashed "bus broken, expect delays."

No, no, no, I turned the radio from Alternative rock to Sinatra's channel. An attempt to calm me.

Sitting on the bridge, not moving an inch, I began daydreaming. I glanced down and noticed my feet were bare. I flashed on loading the car. In all the craziness, did I load my boots in the car? I put the boots by the door. I'm sure I did. Right? Now, my heart was racing for a different reason.

My empty stomach didn't react well to the thought of ushering a San Francisco show barefoot. I wish I could ease my heart rate and jump out of this car and check my damn trunk.

The terror brought on a hot flash. Great. My hair started to frizz under the heat pouring off my body. My face turned beet red. I glanced in the rearview mirror and shook my head at the wide-eyed maniac staring back at me.

My thoughts raced. Did I grab Danny's ATM card? I know I had little cash. Did I have enough to buy shoes and pay for the parking garage? Are there any shoe stores on Valencia St.?

The traffic sucked all the way to the parking garage. I could hear my heart beating. That couldn't be good. That fourth cup of coffee was a mistake. A bad mistake.

My upper lip was sweating as I pulled into the garage. Why is the garage so full? It's never this full. I only had ten minutes until I was expected at the Marsh Theatre.

I found the one spot left in the garage. I flung open the door and jumped out of the car like it was on fire. Then, the world stopped. There I stood, in the covered garage, barefoot in a huge puddle of liquid right next to the car door. It's funny how the brain works in a circumstance like this. There I stood in the puddle, frozen. I was in complete denial.

I screamed out, "I'm sure it's just water. I'm sure it's just water. It's not some stranger's pee. It's not."

Just then, an older couple out for a fun night in the City looked over at me standing in the puddle, screaming about pee to no one.

Patrick, the security guard, was making his rounds.

"Are you okay, Laurie?"

I didn't want Patrick to see me barefoot, standing in the mystery puddle. So, I jumped into my husband's company car with dripping feet and rolled down the window.

"I'm fine, Patrick. Couldn't be better."

Clenching my teeth, with five minutes to get to the theatre, I waited until Patrick continued his rounds. Then I jumped over the huge puddle and popped the trunk.

No boots. My heart sank. I opened the passenger seat door and searched through my purse. In the rush, did I forget to grab Danny's ATM card? My chin started to shake. I could feel the tears coming.

I dumped my purse on the seat and found a wadded-up twenty at the bottom of my purse. I looked up to the sky and thanked the heavens above. I knew parking would be fifteen or sixteen dollars. I scrounged some change off the damp car floor. Ugh.

I found two dollars and seventy-eight cents. After parking money, I had six dollars and seventy-eight cents to find shoes and get to the theatre in seven minutes.

I left the garage barefoot, heading to the theater. I'm not sure which was worse, not knowing what liquid my feet had been submerged in or walking through the streets of San Francisco barefoot.

Shoes became the most important thing in my world. Who sells shoes for six dollars in San Francisco? I ran past the garage cashier and out into the dirty streets of San Francisco.

The first thing I see is a bike messenger spit three times on the sidewalk. Kill me now. That's it; after this fiasco, I'm having the skin on my feet removed. It'll grow back, right?

I ran onto Valencia Street and whipped my head back and forth, looking for a shoe store. There were lots of restaurants, coffee shops, liquor stores, and even a bakery where all the goods were baked from flour made from crickets. But no shoe stores.

Down the block, not far from the theater, I saw a Mexican retail store. They might have flip-flops. I entered the store and heard Mexican music playing. It reminded me of vacation. It brought a smile to my tense face. I did a quick scan of the store and didn't see a shoe in sight.

I did see a huge pinata of Trump, as big as my car, dressed as a baby. Oh, if only I had time to shop. The store was filled with primary-colored items and was an explosion of color. She had every item you could think of except shoes. I ran to the cashier.

"Do you carry flip-flops?"

She tilted her head.

"Flip-flops, shoes?"

She started speaking in Spanish, and this non-speaking Spaniard just shook her head.

"Shoes, I need shoes." I pointed to my feet.

She pointed to the back of the store, where there was a section of socks. I was late for the theater. Socks will have to do. Every pair ranged from fifteen dollars to eighteen.

In the corner, I saw a sale sign. I rifled through the bin. At the bottom was a pair of socks with Frida Kahlo's face all over them. I love Frida. They were colorful and on sale for five dollars and fifty cents. Sold.

The cashier rang me up. "Frida, Bueno." She smiled.

"Si, Frida, muy Bueno." I put the socks on my feet and ran out the door. Of course, I had short capri pants on. I figured my neon Frida socks would create quite a stir on the streets. No one seemed to even notice.

I jay-walked across the street and blew into the theater. Being five minutes late, I ran to the tech booth to apologize to the house manager.

"Sorry, I'm late, Alexa. I had a little trouble getting it together today."

I pointed to my shoeless feet with my festive Frida Kahlo socks on, and we laughed and laughed. I told her the whole ugly story.

That night, I escorted people to their seats and worked the concession stand in my Frida socks, and no one said a word. After another great show at the Marsh, I gathered my purse and keys and went to say goodbye to Alexa.

"Alexa, I ran through the streets and ushered all night with these neon Frida socks, and not one person mentioned it."

Without missing a beat, Alexa said, "Oh, Laurie, you'd have to go to the middle of Mission Street, pull down your pants, and poop to get people's attention. It's the City, girl."

Walking back to my car with my Frida socks protecting me from the horrors on the street, I felt a bond with my Frida socks. I thought as soon as I got home, I would toss those socks and scrub my feet for a few hours.

I entered the house and pulled the socks off. I held them over the garbage can for a few minutes. Then I tossed them into the washer on hot. I'll wash them a few dozen times. They'll be fine.

I couldn't bear to throw my Frida socks away. When I see them in my sock drawer, I smile at them like I would an old friend. Frida and I had been through some shit together.

# Kentucky Fried Covid

Five months into Covid, the scariest thing I'd lived through, I felt like I was losing my marbles. Walking out of my sister's house, I fell and broke my leg on one side and sprained it on the other side. I spent the summer in bed with my leg elevated, watching the shit show that was 2020.

I'm a proud vegetarian who eats the occasional fair hot dog or bacon at Christmas. Don't judge. It's unbecoming. I guess you would call me a flexitarian.

The news this particular night had been nuts. This vegetarian had a mad craving for a Kentucky Fried Chicken original recipe leg. Who am I kidding? It's COVID-19; three Kentucky Fried Chicken original recipe legs.

In early fall, I had started to use crutches.

"Sue, be careful. Crutches are for young people," my Aunt Ann had said.

I learned this the hard way. I had three more substantial falls on my laminate flooring. I was scared to leave the bed. The thought of driving scared me. This Kentucky Fried Chicken, original recipe craving, had taken over my whole body. Clark, my husband, was sleeping. The next day would be a long, stressful day for him. I couldn't wake him for two or three Kentucky Fried Chicken legs.

I crawled out of bed and grabbed my evil crutches. Since COVID, I have lost what little vanity I had. One day, during COVID and the leg incident, I hopped past a mirror and let out a shriek when I saw my reflection in the mirror. I wear a sleep mask at night. Mascara was running down half my face. My hair was dirty and standing at attention. My clothes were stained. I was a hot mess.

This night was no different. Since COVID, I had taken to just throwing on my big furry black coat over my pajamas whenever I had to leave the house for doctor visits. I looked in the mirror and just laughed.

I started on my expedition for Kentucky Fried legs. I hobbled to the front door. I glanced at the mirror and just shook my head in embarrassment. Oh well, I can put a mask on and hide my face. I'm just zipping through the drive-thru.

I threw my big furry black coat over my pajama top. I had no pajama pants on. It's okay, I thought. The coat is big and long. It's dark out, and the neighbors are sleeping. I put my keys in my mouth and hopped out to the car. Fifteen minutes, and I'd be back in bed with my Kentucky Fried legs.

I wobbled to the car, threw my evil crutches in the back seat, and toppled into the front seat. I hadn't driven in months. I was already out of breath, and I hadn't even left the driveway. I tilted the rear-view mirror so I couldn't see my face.

The Kentucky Fried Chicken by our house was a tight U-shaped drive-thru. I pulled up and placed my order right away.

"Great, this should be fast," I said to myself. Yes, since COVID, I have taken to talking to myself out loud. Again, don't judge.

There were three cars ahead of me. I turned Stern on the radio and waited. I waited and waited. What's going on? It's been fifteen minutes, and there's been no movement.

By this time, three cars had pulled up behind me. What is happening? I looked insane. Please, give me my Kentucky Fried original recipe legs, and let me get the hell out of here. I started to get claustrophobic. My heart rate was increasing.

The two women in the two cars ahead of me were out of their cars and talking to each other. I tried to read their lips to figure out what was happening. I sure couldn't get out of the car with no pants on. The women's heads were going back and forth, and fingers were waving around. Crap. This can't be good.

At last, the Kentucky Fried Chicken worker came out. I stuck my dirty hair head out the window to hear what she was saying.

"There's a man at the drive-thru window who won't leave. He says we got his order wrong, but we didn't. We gave him extra chicken, and he still won't budge. We'll keep trying. I'm so sorry for the inconvenience." The Kentucky fried worker slinked back into the store.

Another twenty-five minutes had passed. The two ladies in front of me were still out of their cars, talking to each other. They had plenty of time to establish a deep friendship. I lost it.

"Ladies, it's America. One of you fine Americans must have an assault rifle in one of your trunks. Time to pull it out and shoot behind his tires. Let's get this thing going."

The eyes of both the women in front of me got as big as half dollars. The ladies stopped bobbing their heads and jumped into their respective cars.

"What, everyone's a judge these days? I hate COVID." I pounded my head against the steering wheel.

Another fifteen minutes had passed. I had to pee, and crazy thoughts started to enter my mind. Sue, I thought, just leave the company car in this drive-thru, grab your crutches, and hop down one freeway exit toward your house. Someone will pick you up and take you back home. Home, sweet home.

The Kentucky Fried Chicken worker reappeared. "Okay, I'm going to direct you guys while you back out of the drive-thru."

Crap, I didn't bring my glasses. I didn't think I'd be backing up through a tight U-shaped drive-thru.

The Kentucky Fried worker stopped the traffic in front of the store and guided the two cars out of the drive-thru. Now, it was my turn.

"It's my husband's company car, and I don't have my glasses with me. Please help me, Kentucky Fried worker."

"Don't worry, ma'am, I'll guide you. No problem."

Like tonight hasn't been bad enough. The Kentucky Fried bitch called me ma'am. Kill me now.

I was successful in not denting the company car. I felt free again. Without any Kentucky Fried Chicken in my car and at a very slow pace, I rolled past the front of the

Kentucky Fried Chicken building as the Kentucky Fried worker stood there screaming, "So sorry, ma'am. So sorry, ma'am." I waved with a grimace on my face.

I rolled past the drive-thru window and glared at the maniac still sitting at the window, refusing to leave. I yelled with my dirty hair blowing in the wind, "You're so damn lucky I don't have any pants on, man."

I sped away, chicken-less.

# The Joys of Gardening

"Hi, Janice; thanks for leaving the gate open."

"Sure, Jules, did you bring your swimsuit?"

"Hell yes, it's hot."

"What were you doing? You look all hot and sweaty."

"I was just giving hand jobs to the sunflowers."

"Excuse me? What are you talking about? I'm not sure I want to know the answer."

"Jules, the sunflowers are six or seven feet tall. Over time, all the leaves on the bottom of the sunflowers turn brown and die, hence the hand jobs."

"Sorry, I just never heard it referred to like that."

Jules looked disturbed.

"Jules, hand jobs are a big part of a gardener's life. It's unspoken, but every great gardener knows this. It's common knowledge, Jules, jeez."

"Okay, Janice, whatever you say. I know

now why I'm not a gardener. I'm a good Catholic girl."

"With dead leaves in your garden," I said with a smile.

## My Pinto Was A Badass

My first car was kelly green. She was a Pinto and a badass. I was the fourth owner in our family.

Almost ten years younger than my two older sisters, I watched the Pinto be handed down from my mother to my older sister, Claire, to my middle sister, Kara.

When I turned sixteen, Dad sat me down. "Nicole, you're working now and going to school. You need a car. Would you like to buy the Pinto from us?"

My father didn't believe in buying teenagers cars. He thought it was a great opportunity to teach us about adulthood by working hard to pay for what we need in this world.

"Yes, I want to buy the Pinto. How much? Remember, we're family."

"Three hundred and fifty dollars." We shook on it and the deal was done.

Three hundred and fifty dollars was a lot of money in the 70's. I was confident I could raise the money with my new job at McDonald's, a mile away from the house. To have my own car meant freedom.

So, I would ask my manager, who was nineteen, for more hours so I could buy my sister's badass Pinto. And I thought I might be able to talk Dad down on the price."

"I'm happy to pay the three hundred and fifty dollars, Dad, but you do realize Mom had three wrecks in the Pinto, Claire had two wrecks, and Kara dented every quarter panel on the Pinto."

"Nicole, the Pinto has character. You're lucky I'm giving you this opportunity. That's the price."

I admired Dad's mad negotiating skills. I took on more hours at McDonald's, where my teenage manager's favorite phrase was, "If you can lean, you can clean."

First, I had to learn how to drive. I remember Dad had little patience with me when he tried to help me with math, so I thought I'd ask Mom to teach me.

The Pinto was a stick shift. "Okay, Nicole, I'll teach you to drive, but I still think your dad is the better choice."

Mom took me to a dentist's office parking lot. The lot had a slight slant. Mom pulled over, and we switched places.

"Okay, check your mirrors. Always put your seatbelt on."

"Left foot on the clutch and right foot on the gas."

"Put it in first gear and ease your foot off the clutch while you ease the gas pedal down." Sounded easy enough.

Two hours later, I killed the engine at least one hundred times, throwing Mom forward each time. A stick shift wasn't as easy as I'd thought. Every time I killed the engine, we'd laugh and laugh until tears streamed down our faces. We had a lot of fun, but I was no better at driving. I needed Dad.

Dad took me to the local mall and had me driving in an hour.

I grew up on a long street filled with lots of kids. Being the only kid on the block with my own car, I'd take off in the morning, pick up all the neighborhood kids going to high school, and pack them into the Pinto.

Mom and Dad installed a great stereo system in the Pinto on my sixteenth birthday. The neighbor kids were all surprised when they'd pile into the beat-up

Pinto and discovered it had a badass sound system.

A year later, my older sister, Claire, bought a kicky neon orange Pinto.

I don't mean to brag, but we were now a two-Pinto family.

I owned that Pinto for three glorious years. Other than oil changes, the only attention she ever needed was two brake pads.

Mechanics wasn't my dad's strong suit. Dad would give the Pinto tune-ups. He'd take me out to the garage when he was finished.

"Okay, turn her on. How does it feel?"

I'd start her up, and the Pinto would make this horrible sound so loud I couldn't hear Dad's questions. "How does it feel?" Dad would yell.

"What'd you say, Dad?"

"How does it feel?"

"I can't hear you, Dad."

"Okay. Sounds good." And Dad would walk back into the house, and I'd laugh and laugh. He meant well.

Last fall, I attended my high school reunion, and as it turns out, my badass Pinto meant a lot to my girlfriends, too. The Pinto brought us to high school parties, the lake on the weekends, and out to Briones Park so we could flirt with boys.

Mom let me take my first solo trip to visit Claire, who was now living at Lake Tahoe. I drove ninety miles an hour to Tahoe that day, with one stop at the McDonald's drive-through. If my mother wasn't dead, that last sentence would've killed her.

The Pinto died in Fremont on my way to a job. Dad had it towed to the house and sold it for parts. When the new owner towed it away, I cried as Mom and Dad comforted me. I felt like I was losing a family member -- a dented, reliable family member.

My badass Pinto will forever live in my heart.

# Airport Antics

My friend Sela was a kick to travel with. Sela would insist we arrive at the airport with hours to spare. We'd grab our boarding passes and head to the coffee shop.

"Okay, Fran, enjoy your coffee. I'll be in the bookstore. Want some candy for the trip?"

"No, thanks."

I'd watch Sela saunter into the store that carries books, candy, and magazines. She'd browse over the books, and when she saw an author she deemed evil, Sela would glance at the cashier, smile, grab four books from the display of the evil offender, as she called them, take the books to the very back of the store and put them face down on the shelf nearest to the floor.

While moving through the store, Sela would keep the books low, next to her thigh, so the cashier wouldn't notice her antics. Then, she would repeat the process until most of the evil offender's books were in the back.

Between the trips back and forth, Sela would pick up some knickknack, a shot glass, or a trinket from a local artist and study it with intensity.

"Excuse me, how much is this?" She'd ask the cashier. Then Sela would resume her mission.

Then she'd find another book or two by authors she felt were worthy of a display in the front of the store, where constant foot traffic was a plus. She would repeat the process. She'd take three or four books, hold them below her waist, and go back and forth to the front of the store until she had exchanged enough books for her new displays.

In the middle of this process, Sela would pick up a random book, read the front cover, smile at the cashier, and resume her work.

By the third time I'd traveled with Sela, she had the routine down. I sat in the coffee shop across from the bookstore that Sela had targeted. While sipping my coffee, I watched Sela move through the store. Watching her was like watching a choreographed dance.

Sela's speed had improved since we last traveled together. Her whole mission was completed in five or six minutes. Then she ran from the bookstore back to my table in the coffee shop like a kid on the last day of school.

"Fran, take a picture of me with my displays; hurry before the cashier notices."

As I snatched my backpack off my chair, she grabbed my elbow and led me to her displays.

"Are you sure we should stack the books you moved and spread one open for show? Aren't you tempting fate?"

But Sela is a daredevil and was proud of her work. Then she stood right between her two new displays. Her hands akimbo, one hand pointing toward Tina Fey's new book and the other hand pointing toward Chelsea Handler's latest book. She smiled like a Cheshire cat as I took her picture.

"Fran, I'm going to grab some coffee. Be right back."

I sauntered to the back of the bookstore and there were two huge stacks of Bill O'Reilly's books facedown near the floor. I laughed looking at Sela's work.

As Sela and I walked through the crowded airport, I asked, "How long have you been moving book displays at airport bookstores?"

"Oh, since the eighties when I was a kid. I guess it's my little way of making the world a better place."

"It's always good to give back, Sela."

Sela ran ahead to the escalator and yelled back, "Come on, Fran. There are two more bookstores downstairs. Step it up."

# Dad

Spring was here, which meant Dad and I had a lot of work to do in the yard. I just turned eight, and I was quite the tomboy. My two older sisters were much more feminine than myself.

My sisters, Gwen and Sandy, would walk up to Dad in his garden with their frilly dresses on and twirl their hair.

"Dad, could you drive us to Debbi Borhink's house?"
Dad would stop what he was doing and grab his keys. My sisters had Dad under their thumbs.

I, too, had Dad under my thumb, but I had my own things with Dad. After Dad and I would take care of whatever work the garden and fruit trees needed, we would play my favorite game.

Dad and I would go to the gate on the side of the house, next to Gwen's bedroom window, and I would look at Dad, take the stance of an Olympic runner, and I'd scream, "Say go, Dad."

Dad would check his watch and scream, "Go."

I would jump on the gate, climb up onto the roof, and run across the length of the house. I would stretch my little eight-year-old leg out until I reached the gate outside the kitchen window, and Dad would give me my time for that day.

Dad and I played this game for months until one day, I was so intent on beating the prior day's time that I fell flat on my face. I got up fast and continued running across the roof. I jumped down to the gate and slid down the fence to the ground.

Dad was standing at the gate, ready to give me that day's time. Just then, Mom came around the corner. Her eyes were big, and she had a spatula in her hand.

"George, Tina, what the hell was that thump on the roof? I'm cooking dinner, and I jumped when I heard that thud on the roof."

I looked up at Dad. I figured I was too young to address this. I'd let Dad take the question. Mom seemed upset.

"Sue, well, see, Tina, likes to climb up the fence, run across the roof, and climb down the other gate while I time her. You know, see if she could beat yesterday's time."

"George, you 've done this before?"

"Sure, Mom, we've done it for months."

Dad looked at me like I had just turned him in to the police.

"George, she's eight, and you're encouraging her to run faster on the roof? What the hell, George."

"Well, honey, she's really good at it. She gets faster every day."

"Oh my God, George. This game is over. If I hear your little feet on the roof, I'll put you both on restriction."

Dad giggled. I looked up at him, and we made eye contact as Mom turned the corner to get back to cooking dinner. Mom was shaking her head and mumbling under her breath. Dad gave me a sly look, and I knew I'd be back on our roof.

The next day, the game had changed. Now, the game was even more exciting because we had to go check where Mom was and make sure Mom was busy making dinner.

Dad and I would hide under the kitchen window, and Dad would whisper when he saw Mom had left the stove and begun setting the table for dinner. I would climb up the gate and tiptoe across the roof. The smells coming out of the vent on the roof would tell me what we were having for dinner.

On the other side of the house, I would climb down from the roof as quietly as a mouse and jump down the fence.

Dad and I played this game for years. Mom was never the wiser.

And people wonder why I don't have kids. Really?

# Troy the Cat

The heat wave was relentless. Our small bay community could only take so many days with temperatures over one hundred.

I was a junior in high school. My boyfriend, Troy, was on his way over. I heard a knock on the door.

"Hey Troy,"

"Hey, Trish. Alex and Phil are in the car. Want to take a drive out to the valley and get away from this heat?"

"You know I do. I hate the heat."

Alex and Phil were boys from the neighborhood. We all grew up together. Phil was a habitual liar, so he was fun to watch. Phil would lie about silly stuff and big stuff. He lied so often I don't think he even realized how much he lied.

We all lived in a small farming community in the suburbs. Past our high school, there were miles of wooded area before you reached another town. The teenagers of our town loved to meet up out in the valley and party.

In high school, they showed us horrible movies of car wrecks out in the valley to deter kids from using the windy roads as our personal race tracks.

"Phil, get the hell in the backseat. Let Trish sit in front."

"Why, Trish is so much smaller than me? I can't get my tall ass legs in the back of this Volkswagen."

"Shut up and get in the back," Troy barked.

Thank goodness my boyfriend was the alpha male in our group. Fibber Phil rolled his eyes and began cramming his lanky legs in the back of the Volkswagen.

"I have boobs, Phil, and you don't. Backseat it is, buddy." I smiled as I held the front seat for Phil to get in the back.

We had all the windows rolled down, desperate for a respite from the heat. Led Zepplin blared as we cruised through the dark valley.

The three boys were talking their usual teen boy stuff. I listened, giggling under my breath. Troy had pulled off the road under a tree so the boys could smoke a joint. I didn't smoke, but I loved when they did. Their conversations became even more entertaining.

"Do you think a person could live off of Doritos Nacho Cheese chips for a year?" Alex asked.

"Hell no, think what their poop would look like." Phil laughed.

"Do you think the poop would be orange?" Troy asked.

"I hate to break into this Mensa group meeting, but what the hell is that white thing outside the car?" I asked.

"Where, what are you talking about?" Asked Troy.

"Over there, by that bush," I yelled.

With the lights of the Volkswagen off, the night was pitch black except for this little white spot moving around.

"Oh ya, I see it. It's a kitten." Alex said.

"A kitten? That kitten can't survive out here with all these wild animals. Some dumbass dumped it. Troy, get that kitten for me, please, Troy." I begged.

Troy whipped his neck around and looked at fibber Phil.

"Phil, you heard her; go get that kitten."

"No way, man. I'm allergic to cats." We all knew Phil's mom had three cats. Fibber Phil strikes again.

"Get your ass out of the car and get that kitten." The alpha had spoken. Phil finagled his lanky legs out of the backseat of the two-door Volkswagen.

Phil glared at me as he ventured out into the pitch-black night. I wrinkled my nose and smiled at Troy. For being well over six feet, Phil was a big ol' chicken.

We all coaxed Phil from the car.

"She's over there now, under that bush. Grab her, Phil." Alex yelled.

You could tell Phil was scared. He kept looking around and jumping every time he heard a wild animal. I so enjoyed this. Phil wasn't the most likable character in the neighborhood.

"She's right there, Phil. Grab her." Alex screamed.

Phil bent down and grabbed the kitten. The kitten went nuts on Phil's arms, scratching like a maniac, trying to escape Phil's grasp on her. I felt like I was watching a Looney Tunes Cartoon. Fibber Phil and the kitten rolled on the dirt. The kitten let out a primal scream, and so did fibber Phil. It was quite the dust-up.

"She doesn't want to come. Let me in the damn car."

"Not without the kitten, Phil. Them's the rules." Alex was laughing so hard tears were running down his face.

Alex threw his sweatshirt out the window. Phil grabbed it and wrapped the kitten in the hood of the jacket. I jumped out of the car and pushed the seat up for Phil.

Phil pretty much pushed the kitten into my chest and flopped into the backseat.

The kitten was so cute, she had black and white fur.

"That was messed up, man. I got scratches all over my arms from that damn cat."

"So, Phil, this three-pound kitten really had its way with you, huh?" I asked, giggling.

Laughter filled the Volkswagen. The laughter and ribbing of fibber Phil lasted all the way to town.

"Stop at the seven-eleven. I'll get the kitten some food. Poor thing looks hungry."

I jumped out of the car and started to hand Phil the kitten.

"No way, man. No way." I handed her to Alex.

I bought the kitten the diet of teenagers. Beef jerky and Doritos Nacho Cheese chips. She seemed to really enjoy the food.

Troy dropped the boys at their respective houses and proceeded to mine. I couldn't wait until Monday to hear Phil's account of the evening. I'm sure fibber Phil's scratches will be from a lion or a Wildebeest and not a three-pound kitten.

"Do you think your dad will let you keep the kitten?" Troy asked as he kissed me goodnight.

"Well, I think I'll wait until tomorrow and we'll have an adult conversation."

"Good luck with that," Troy said as he sped off. I tucked the small kitten in my jacket on the left side so Dad wouldn't spot her. Our dad had a habit of sleeping on the couch in the living room until all three of his girls were home safe and in bed.

I walked in and turned my head to the right to see Dad awaken from his nap.

"Home, Dad. I'm just going to put my purse away. Be right back."

I scurried down the hall to my bedroom. My room was right across the hall from Mom and Dad's room. Mom was fast asleep. As quiet as a mouse, I put the kitten on my bed.

"Okay, no meowing, got it?"

I shut the door tight and returned to the living room.

"Did you guys have fun?" Dad asked.

"Ya, we just took a ride out to the valley to escape the heat. I hate this heat, Dad. The trees in the valley cooled us off. I hope the heat wave is over soon, Dad."

I sat on a chair on one side of the living room, and Dad was on the couch on the opposite side. The next thing I knew, the kitten walked into the living room and sat right in the middle between Dad and me.

The kitten looked up at me, then turned her head and looked at Dad. The silence seemed to last an hour. My easygoing dad's eyes looked like coasters.

"Did ya get a cat, Dad? She's a cutey." Dad looked at me, trying not to laugh, and said, "Trish, that cat goes to the shelter in the morning, understand?"

"Understand, Dad. Sleep well." I picked up the kitten and cowered to my bedroom. That night, I named the kitten Troy after my boyfriend. Troy didn't get her for me, but he did expedite the capture.

Troy, the kitten, slept with me that night.

Troy stayed with my parents long after I had moved out. Troy brought us many years of joy and laughter. You could always find Troy on my Dad's lap or on the couch next to him. My mother had taken to calling Troy dad's furry wife.

## Carol F*!#!n Burnett

I woke up to my husband handing me a Mother's Day card. Even though my husband, Sam, and I have no children, we've had pug dogs for over twenty years. We have always exchanged gifts and cards on Mother's Day and Father's Day.

Our beloved pug, Rocky Hudson, had just passed after fifteen wonderful years with us.

"Here, sweetie. Happy Mother's Day." Sam handed me the card.

2020 was no different for us; we had lost family, friends, and Rocky. I broke my leg, blah, blah, blah. We were so happy to welcome 2021 and here I was opening a Mother's Day card.

"Aw, thanks boo, I didn't expect a Mother's Day card this year." I opened the card and it read - Happy Mother's Day from our future baby. I wiped the tears from my eyes, and we hugged.

This lit a fire in me. A puppy is just what this house needs. I wanted to rescue a dog. We really missed the crazy antics of pugs. For most of my life, I'd rescued cats and I felt getting a dog was the right thing to do. Sam worked next to a dog rescue. I would meet Sam at the rescue facility at Sam's lunchtime. We spent months "test" walking dogs.

One day, I met Sam at the shelter, and we went "test" walking with a very sweet, long-haired mutt. The dog was much bigger than what I wanted. Small dog, small poop; right?

The hot sun beamed down on our backs as we started our walk. We turned a corner, and another prospective dog owner was also walking a shelter dog. I held on tight, not yet knowing the temperament of this particular dog.

The tight grip didn't help. The sweet dog stood up on two legs and let out a yelp. Before I knew it, I was on the ground with the leash wrapped around me, and Sam was running down the street, trying to catch the dog. I sat on the ground, covered in the dog's long, white hair.

Sam came back with the dog and helped me up off the ground.

"We're Pug People. Who are we kidding?" Sam said. I agreed, and the search for a baby pug began.

A couple of days later, I met this nice couple at the park with a baby pug. She gave me the number of their breeder.

I thought about calling the breeder but felt guilty about buying a dog. I've brought no children into this overpopulated world. I recycle. I eat organic. Please, humans, let me have this one indiscretion.

"What do you think, Sam? Should I call this woman about her pugs?"

"Yes, call her. It's too quiet in this house. I need the sound of a dog in the house. We tried to rescue Anita. Like I said, we're Pug People."

It was Mother's Day, and being I had lost my mom some twenty years ago, I really wanted to make this happen. I missed Rocky, and I missed my mom.

"Okay, the breeder says she has one girl left. Another family is coming to see her tomorrow at four. I'll have to be there in the morning."

I needed to see the girl dog. I don't want a boy. Picking up your dog and having a hand full of pug penis, no thank you.

Sam had a bunch of deals happening at work that he couldn't neglect, so I was on my own. I had attended my beloved literary agent's funeral the day before Mother's Day, and I was fragile, to say the least.

The funeral had been a four-hour drive there and back. My healing broken leg wasn't ready for yet another long drive. Like my mom, I was horrible at directions. If Mom said left, you knew it was a right turn.

"Where's Elk Grove," I asked Sam. "That's where the breeder lives. Think I can find it?"

"Sure, bring your phone. The weather news says there will be strong winds in all the towns you'll be driving through. I wish I could go with you."

"You and me both, buddy."

The next morning, I had a tight knot in my stomach. Please, heavens above, let me pick up my puppy without incident. Please, let me get to our front door with the new puppy with no trauma. I do not want a story for a future book. I'm too fragile.

I threw the crate for the new puppy in my truck, and off I went. The news hadn't exaggerated; the winds were crazy. The whole truck rattled. I held onto the steering wheel for dear life. My twenty-year-old truck felt like it would tip over any second.

Much to my surprise, I found the breeder's house with no trouble.

I sat in my car, wondering what the hell I was doing. Here I am in some strange farming community, meeting a stranger on Craigslist with a pocket full of money. I saw the movie *Craigslist Killer*. Stranger, danger.

I lived by or in Richmond for decades, and growing up, on weekends, I stayed at both my grandma's houses in Oakland. I had the cash in one pocket and an open buck knife in the other pocket. Just in case she was the killer.

Before I left, I asked the breeder on the phone why her pugs were one thousand and others were as much as three thousand.

"My pugs are not AKC, so you can't show them at dog shows. They are the way pugs are meant to be. Over the years, breeders have bred pugs to have smashed noses and other bad characteristics. That's why they have respiratory issues. My pugs are real pugs." The breeder had said with defiance.

This made me feel much better. I knocked on the breeder's door. I surveyed her front courtyard to plan my escape if necessary. A sweet young woman answered the door and handed me the tinniest pug I'd ever seen. She had a huge protruding stomach.

"What's with her stomach?" I asked the woman.

"She just ate. She's a really good eater."

I thought, has there ever been a pug that wasn't a good eater? The tiny pug fit in my hand. The poor thing shook like crazy. The breeder gave me her health records and some food for the day.

I named her Carol Burnett after one of my comedy idols. I put Carol in the crate in the front seat with me. I had the opening of the crate facing me so Carol could see me on the way home. She was a nervous little baby.

I somehow found my way back to the freeway. Poor Carol was shaking, looking up at me. Poor baby. Carol had just left her five siblings and her birth mother. Here she sat, rattling around in my old truck with the winds howling.

I looked over at Carol in the crate and saw her do a complete somersault. I laughed my obnoxious laugh, and Carol's eyes were big, and she howled. I guess Carol's birth mom didn't have a laugh that could stop traffic. I tried my best not to laugh the rest of the journey.

Carol and I pulled up to the house, and I felt a sense of calm wash over me. My bad leg had held up, and my old truck made the journey. The heavens above listened to me. We had made it home safely, without incident.

The excitement of showing Carol Burnett her new home was overwhelming. I picked up her crate, opened the door, and sat baby Carol in the entryway of her new house.

"Okay, Baby Carol, I've got to get you a few things at the store. I'll be right back, and then I'll show you around."

I set the alarm and jumped in the truck. I flew to the store, got what Carol needed, and rushed home. I couldn't wait to play with our new baby.

I jumped out of the truck and stuck my key in the door and the key broke off in the lock. No, man, no. My heart raced. No problem, my neighbor, Rachael, has a key. I ran across the street. No Rachael. Crap.

I ran back to my house and got on the retaining wall by the gate. I pulled myself up and climbed the six-foot fence. Thank goodness I do Pilates. I'm too old for these shenanigans.

Growing up, I watched our neighborhood's shady boys go to any of our friend's houses when their parents were at work, and they would lift the sliding glass door right off the tracks. Then, we'd have a party, and afterward, the shady boys would replace the sliding glass door. We'd leave, and the parents were none the wiser.

I really didn't want to call my husband at work on a busy Monday. I thought of those shady neighborhood boys. I ran to the sliding glass door in the back of the house. I lifted the sliding glass door and tried to jimmy it off the tracks. Well, it turns out they make sliding doors better than they did in the 70's. The door wouldn't open, but it did set off the loudest alarm I'd ever encountered.

My blood pressure spiked. I started shaking. Poor Carol was stuck in her crate with the alarm blaring. Welcome to your new home, Carol. I climbed back over the fence to the front yard.

With my hands shaking like a leaf, I called a locksmith.

"Sure, lady, I could be there in a couple of hours."

"No sir, you don't understand, I have a baby alone in the house."

I looked up to see two police cars rolling up in front of the house. They jumped out and pulled their guns out.

"This is my house, don't shoot. I live here, and the key broke off in the lock." The cops, cute cops, I might add, returned their guns to their holsters.

"Does one of you happen to have needle nose pliers on you?"

The coppers and I had to scream to speak to each other over the loud alarm. One of the cute cops opened one of the many pockets on the front of his uniform and pulled out a tiny pair of needle nose pliers. This guy must've been a Boy Scout.

"You mean like this one?" He said with pride. I could tell this kid wanted to be a hero. By all means, kid, be my hero. The cop stuck the pliers in the keyhole, turned the broken key, and opened the door.

I turned off the alarm and looked in the crate. Carol Burnett's eyes were as big as tires. She looked at me as if to say, "Bitch, let me out of this cage. I'm running back to Elk Grove. This is not working out."

The neighbors had gathered in front of the house. Just then a fire truck pulled up with its lights on and Sam came flying around the corner like the original Steve McGarrett on the old *Hawaii 5-0*. I guess the alarm company had called him. Thanks so much.

"Cancel the locksmith," I screamed to my husband as I fell to the ground in a sobbing heap on the driveway, like one of Trump's advisers.

Be careful how you word your desires; I did make it to the front door without incident, as I'd requested. Damn.

After the dust had settled, the cops and the fire truck left, the neighbors went back home, and my disgruntled husband returned to work, Carol Burnett and I took a long nap.

Carol Burnett is two years old now. Our third pug is different from our first two, Doris Day and Rocky Hudson. Carol loves to tumble. I tried to find her a Gymboree class to no avail. The other mothers didn't want poor Carol in their classes. New moms can be so cliquey.

Carol loved to eat her poop during her first year with us. I found this very disturbing. I'd never had a dog that ate her poop. That spring, I brought home a bag of double doody manure for gardening. I dropped the heavy doody bag on the back patio, and Carol smelled it. Carol looked like a kid who just got a bike at Christmas.

As I spread the double doody over the yard, Carol ran like a bat out of hell to all the plants I'd spread the doody over. She looked up at me with a face full of doody, and the girl was in heaven.

Sometimes at night, I'll get up to pee and see Carol skulking around, looking very guilty. She'll put her funny face around the hall corner, and I could see a little bit of poop on the corner of her mouth, and I'd know she'd been up to no good.

Carol has had more suicide attempts than both of the other pugs combined. Carol eats succulents in the backyard, and she acts like she's on an acid trip. The first year was just about keeping this bitch alive.

I spent a good portion of the first year chasing her around the backyard, pulling stuff out of her mouth. What my neighbor behind us must think. I seemed to always be running after her, screaming, "Carol Burnett, why are you such a dick?" I should've named her Wednesday or Linda Blair.

My dad was old school. Dad believed dogs belonged in the backyard, rain or shine. I laugh, thinking what Dad must think, looking down from heaven and seeing Carol's carpeted stairs to our bed or her expensive probiotics.

Carol's having a deep love affair, on our couch, with our leopard print pillow. She's spicy. On any given day, I'll be cooking in the kitchen and hear rigorous lovemaking coming from the living room. I'll look around the corner, and she'll have the leopard print pillow on the ground, having her way with it.

Carol has eaten every bed we've bought her. She tears them to sheds. She's on her eighth bed. I was worried about the leopard print pillow in the living room. I broke down and bought her yet another bed in the hopes that she would break up with the leopard print couch pillow.

Carol's new bed didn't help. She just two-timed the couch pillow with her new bed. Carol Burnett is loose. It's hump city around here.

Carol's a growler. She can be quite evil if you attempt to take her bed or a toy away. Lookout. Carol doesn't mess around. She'll growl, and her eyes roll to the back of her head. All eight pounds of her have been known to push me backward into our bedroom as she growls at me.

Our friend, Karla, runs a very successful dog-sitting and dog-training facility. When Karla visits, she looks at crazy Carol and says, in a sweet voice, "Maybe Carol should spend some time with me? What'd you think?"

Baby Carol has bitten me twice. I've tried to be firm with her, but she only gets madder. I, too, am stubborn. I'm shorter than my two sisters, and Carol was the tinniest pug in the litter. Sam says that's our problem. Two runts going at it.

Because Carol's not AKC, she has a nice, big nose to breathe out of, and she has the shortest feet I've ever seen on a dog. I'm surprised she doesn't fall forward. I've taken to calling her Stubs.

Sam doesn't care for the name Stubs. My English mother-in-law, Fay, now calls her Stubs, which Sam hates. Sam will be at his mother's house with Carol, and much to his chagrin, his mother, who loves Carol, will call Carol in her English accent, "ello Stubs, would you like a biscuit?"

When I do my daily yoga, Stubs, or Carol, if you will, always waits until I do the child pose and she'll stick her cute face under my arm and kiss my face. Carol is the sweetest and meanest pug we've had. I've learned she's just a growler. All bark and a little bite.

We adore our little maniac. When Carol does one of her weird or strange things, Sam and I look at each other and say,

"Well, we know why Carol was one thousand instead of three thousand, don't we."

# The Night J. J. was Born

Summer was in full gear. The phone rang. I'm not a phone person, but my niece was pregnant, and she could pop at any second. So I ran to answer the call.

"She's in labor," my sister, Mia, screamed.

"Yay. I'm on my way."

"Come to Tara's house. We'll stay here until Tara calls us to go to the hospital. This could take a while."

My beautiful niece, Tara, and her wonderful partner, Eric, were expecting their first. The baby would be my sister's first grandchild. This was a special baby and the family was over the moon.

Jay's birth would be the third labor room I had been blessed to be in. Experiencing labor is one of the most beautiful experiences on this planet. Nothing I'd ever want to experience, but cool for you guys.

Tara had wanted a baby for years, and through the miracles of IVF, she got her baby.

I had been in the room when Mia gave birth to Tara years prior. This made Jay's birth extra special for me.

I didn't grab lunch or dinner that Friday. After the call from Mia, I was busy throwing things into my backpack for the hospital. By now, I was a pro in hospital labor rooms. I packed water, a phone, candy, and aspirin.

Crossing the Bay Bridge on a Friday afternoon can be challenging. I hoped the traffic would cooperate. I can't miss this baby being born.

"You made good time, Emma. You didn't speed, did you?"

"Me speed, Hell no," I said with a smile.

Tara's couch was very comfortable -- a big L-shape with a chaise lounge on one side. I soon claimed the chaise. We watched *Murders in the Building* while we waited for Mia to call.

Mia received texts from Tara throughout the evening. Tara still wasn't dilated enough to warrant us going to the hospital.

"I think we should sleep here tonight and go to the hospital in the morning," Mia said.

Eric and Tara have a big, beautiful dog and two cute cats. I'm a cat and dog person, so having them around was calming.

"Sounds good, Mia. We'll hit the hospital early."

"I know, it's so exciting. We'll see if we get any sleep."

I'd stopped at the store on the way to Tara's house, but because I hadn't eaten, I made poor choices. I picked up some cheese and crackers and small chocolate cream pies. Come on, Emma, what're you thinking?

Mia had dosed off on her side of the couch. I almost fell asleep when Eric's cat, Betty, jumped on my stomach and started kneading it like a pastry chef making his dough for the day.

I had lost my cat, Bill, so Betty's affection was relished. Betty must've weighed around four pounds. She seemed like a kitten. I would later learn Betty was nineteen. What? I want Betty's Botox doctor's number. Betty looked fabulous.

The sun rose on the beach town. Mia stirred in the kitchen, making coffee.

"Emma, want some coffee?"

"No thanks. I'll get coffee at the hospital."

"Did you sleep, Emma?"

"Betty had her way with me most of the night. No, I didn't sleep much. Betty's a doll. I want to take her home with me."

"How about you? Did you sleep?"

"Yah, I slept a little. Tara just texted, She's dilating. We better get to the hospital."

I had purchased some balloons and flowers for the new parents. I put them in the kitchen so they could see them when they walked in with their new bundle of joy.

I followed Mia to the hospital in my car. I jumped out of my car at the hospital. Mia approached. She looked so excited.

"You know, Mia, those lines on the freeway are not a suggestion."

"Oh, shut up."

We laughed.

Tara was lucky enough to have a private room. When we arrived, Tara was hooked up to the monitoring machines. It all came back to me -- having your eyes glued to the monitors and waiting for the contractions to increase. Eric stood next to Tara, being supportive.

"I'm four centimeters dilated," Tara said with excitement.

I didn't have the heart to tell her first births could take a while.

We all got comfortable. The room had a cubbyhole, and Eric had a blanket and pillow for himself. I thought it was nice that he had a place to lie down. The room also had a rocking chair and a couple of other chairs where Mia and I could relax.

There was little use for the chairs. We were all rubbing Tara's feet and trying to make her comfortable while she did her breathing exercises.

The wonderful nurses and midwife gave us instructions on how to make her breathing help the contractions. Poor Tara, the contractions were hard and long all day. My sister would tell Tara, "Breathe deep, one more time."

During one strong contraction, Mia started to tell Tara how to breathe, and boy, if looks could kill, Tara screamed, and Mia threw her head back in case Tara took a swing at her. You always take it out on the ones you love.

Oh, how I laughed.

I have a lot of nurses in my family. I already knew nurses were angels on earth. The nurses were so impressive to watch. They never stopped turning Tara, taking her vitals, giving her ice chips, and whatever She needed.

The hard contractions lasted throughout the day. The dilation would start, and then the progress would stop.

Eric and Tara had already been at the hospital for almost twenty-four hours. I saw Eric try to sit and rest in the cubbyhole. Tara screamed, "If I can't sleep, buddy, you can't either."

Mia and I just smiled. Watching Tara go through hours of hard contractions was wearing on all of us. I can only imagine how Tara felt.

"Mia, let's go get something to eat. We can bring Eric some dinner." By this time, my stomach was growling. I needed caffeine, and I needed it yesterday.

"Mia, let's check the hospital cafeteria. Most hospitals have pretty good food." Mia and I went downstairs to the cafeteria. It looked like a full-service restaurant, but no one was behind the counter. I saw a cashier in the back.

"Excuse me, when does your cafeteria open?"

"We're closed for the weekend."

Damn. Mia and I picked up some chips and soda and sat outside in the courtyard. "How long do you think the midwife will let her go without suggesting a C-section?" I asked.

"I don't know. Tara really wants to have the baby naturally. Let's go down the street and see if we can find a restaurant and some damn caffeine."

Mia and I walked down the street to find most restaurants closed. We were on a mission to find sustenance.

"You'd think something would be open on a Saturday." We spotted a Starbucks in the distance.

"I see a customer in the window. Run, Mia." Mia tore off like she was running for dear life. This woman needs her caffeine.

"Sorry, we're closed." The Starbucks worker said. Mia and I continued down this weird street until we came to a Mexican restaurant with beautiful décor and a Mariachi band playing in the back.

"Let's get some dinner before we pass out," Mia said. It takes a lot out of a person watching someone you love writhing in pain for hours.

We were seated and began to look at the strangest Mexican food menu I'd ever seen -- lots of strange pairings and lots of mole entrees. I'm sorry, I'm a Hispanic, but I don't want chocolate in my damn entrees. I think the lack of food was beginning to make me cranky.

I only ordered rice and beans. I figured they couldn't screw that up. Poor Mia ordered a full dinner and couldn't eat it at all. We soon realized that's probably why they had a Mariachi band. It might distract you from the crappy food. Mia and I decided to go back to the trenches to see how our girl was doing.

Hours passed while Tara fought through the hardest labor I'd ever witnessed. At one point, around ten in the evening, a night nurse walked in while Tara screamed the "F" word.

"I'm sorry, nurse. I never say that word. I'm a nice person on a regular day."

The nurse smiled at Tara and said, "Oh, Tara, we nurses don't really consider it hard labor until the mother tells their significant other to 'F' off." The room enjoyed a much-needed laugh. We wiped the sweat from poor Tara's red face.

We saw nurses come in on their shifts and finish their shifts. The hours passed. Two of the nurse angels came in, and rolled Tara on a sheet from one side to the other, to try to alleviate her pain. The little stinker's foot was jabbing Tara in her rib.

The midwife said, "I hope you're not modest, Tara, your whole butt is on display for the room. Sorry."

"No problem, nurse. Tara's the only one in our family who has a butt. We're quite proud," I said, laughing.

Mia played John Lennon's song, "Beautiful Boy." The moment was beautiful as we waited for our boy.

It had been my experience that once the mother received the epidural, things went easier. All eyes were on the monitors, hoping the contractions would ease up. Hours passed. We were all worried for Tara. The hard contractions would get strong, and then they'd stop.

The anesthesiologist came in to save the day. He was now giving her meds to make the contractions stronger. More pain meds, more pain meds.

Tara looked exhausted. The doctors would tell us the baby wasn't in harm's way. I just kept thinking of the mortality rate for mothers in the United States. Not good. Tara was about to turn 40. I followed the midwife out of the room.

"How long until you suggest a C-section?" I asked.

"The baby's not in distress, but we won't let her go too much longer."

Tara was up to hour thirty-nine. This all seemed like too much. Two more hours passed, and the excitement had turned to worry. It was so hard watching my sister and Eric look scared.

The room was buzzing with nurses. Tara's Doctor came in.

"Tara, I think it's time to consider a C-section."

Tara burst into tears. She had so wanted to have a vaginal birth. My heart broke for her. The midwife came in to talk.

"Tara, I know you wanted to have this baby your way, but we can only give you the contraction medicine every couple of hours. If you decide to go forward without a C-section, you are in for the most brutal six or seven hours of hard labor you'll ever have.

"Are you up for that?" The midwife asked.

Tara cried. She was now up to hour forty-one. I put my head down. I was terrified. It seemed like too much pain meds, too much trauma. Tara, please say yes to a C-section, I thought.

The maternity doctor, who had no bedside manner, described all the horrible things that could go wrong with a C-section to the frightened Tara and Eric. The darkness of the night seemed to engulf the room.

"I'll leave you so you two can decide what you want to do," the doctor said.

I knew my sister couldn't tell Tara what to do. If something terrible happened, she would have to live with that. I had no problem opening my big mouth.

I whispered to my crying niece, "Tara, I have so many friends and family members who have had C-sections, and I've never heard of any problems."

Tara and Eric looked at each other.

"Tara, you've done such a great job. If you do have the C-section, you can be back in this room in an hour with your baby boy." I begged.

"Let's give the parents some privacy to decide," Mia whispered. I could see the worry on Mia's face.

We all left the room. I walked up to the doctor, Mrs. Personality, who was waiting outside the room,

"Excuse me, Doctor, have you done a lot of C-sections before?" I could tell Mrs. Personality wanted to pop me in the mouth.

"Yes, I've done hundreds of C-sections."

Mrs. Personality turned and walked down the hall.

I hated to see the anguish on Mia's face. We all returned to Tara's room to see what the couple had decided.

"We'll have a C-section," Tara said through her tears.

My stomach dropped. Now we'll have to worry about infection and surgery. I went into the bathroom in Tara's room and dropped to my knees on the hospital floor to pray. It's okay. I'll just throw these pants away when I get home. I'm a recovering Catholic. I got kicked out at nine for asking a question. I hoped the big Kahuna wouldn't hold that against me.

Mia's room was a hotbed of activity. The anesthesiologist put something in the garbage can behind me. I grabbed his hand, "She's going to be okay, right?" I gave him my best Tony Soprano face.

"Yes, she'll be fine." He reassured me.

"If she doesn't have an infection, Eric can come into the surgical room. If she does have an infection, this will be a more extensive surgery, and he won't be allowed in," the doctor informed us.

They whisked Tara off to surgery.

Mia, Eric, and I were the only ones left in the room. No one spoke. We sat in the dark room in quiet terror. I couldn't take it anymore. I walked down to surgery and just stared at the door. I called on all my guardian angels.

It seemed like hours, but, in reality, it was probably twenty minutes. The nurse came out and motioned Eric to go into the room. Oh, thank you, guardians. No infection. Tara will be awake to witness the birth of their baby.

Now, back in the dark room, Mia and I waited. We were silent. I left to go stand in front of the surgical room again.

Then I walked back into Tara's room, and Mia's face said it all. She handed me her phone. I looked down at a picture of Tara, holding the cutest boy I'd ever seen. Tara's hand rested on the baby's chest. I screamed a primal scream and threw my sister's phone across the room.

"Oops, sorry, Sis."

The nurse wheeled Tara back into her room. She had the beautiful boy on her chest. The room was electric. The nurse took the baby from Tara and put him on a tray with lights above him. The nurse gave him a shot in both his legs and rubbed some sort of goo on his eyes. The baby took this all well. Welcome to the world, baby.

The baby was so alert, and he looked like he had muscles. I'd had a lot of friends over the years who've had lots of trouble getting their babies to latch on. "The Boobie Monster," as Mia now refers to him, latched right on.

The nurses were great at training Tara on breastfeeding. After all that Tara had been through, to see the boy healthy and latching on so quickly was heartwarming. A birthing room is so magical.

I hated to leave the situation, but I hadn't eaten or slept much in the last three days, and I knew I had to head back to my side of the Bay. We all hugged, and I walked out of the hospital, exhausted, dazed, and elated.

As I drove over the empty Bay Bridge, the sun was coming up, and I looked up at the heavens and thanked my mom. She had passed almost twenty years ago. I knew she had a hand in this. After forty-three hours of hard labor, we have a funny, happy, healthy baby boy who has brought a new light into our family.

I'm so looking forward to being a part of the Boobie Monster's journey.

## Color Coordination
## Is the Key to a Happy Life

Everybody has gifts. Some people have lots of gifts, some people have a few gifts, and some people have one gift. Some people, well, I'm sure you have a gift. We just haven't found it yet.

One of my gifts was fashion; I read *Glamour Magazine* until I turned eight, then I switched to *Vogue*. At sixteen, I worked at Piccadilly, which was yesteryears Ross.

Working at Piccadilly, I came to the shocking realization that not everyone had good taste in fashion. I worked the morning shift so I could go to college for fashion merchandising and work my restaurant job at night.

At this stage of my career, I'd only worked at Richmond Hilltop Mall, which was almost in my backyard. Not being a morning person did not help with my early shifts. I hadn't yet discovered the joys of caffeine.

To say I was shy in high school would be an understatement. As a shy person, I had no problem being fearless with fashion. I was the first girl in my high school to wear Candie's shoes with a blazer and skinny jeans. The kids pointed and laughed at my fashion choices. Then, six months later, a lot of the kids had abandoned their bellbottoms for skinny jeans and Candie's high heels.

I pretty much slept through the first part of my shift. The morning shift meant a lot of new moms coming into the store with their midgets from hell. Sorry, that's not politically correct. They'd come in with their charming little people.

At the front of the store, there was a turnstile with metal bars making rows for the customers to line up. The turnstiles were often used as a jungle gym by the charming little people the young moms brought in. A good portion of my morning would be spent whisper-yelling to the charming little people on the jungle gym/turnstile.

"How old are you, kid?" I'd ask when my manager wasn't looking.

"I'm five, lady."

I'd whisper yell, "Do you want to be six, kid? Get off the turnstile, now."

Working the morning shift meant I'd open all boxes received that day. I could pull all the size one Jordache Jeans and put them aside before my co-worker, Nan, who was also size one, could get them. Hey, it's every woman for herself at discount clothiers, man.

I soon realized, when I changed from the night shift to the day shift, that being a yard teacher was now in my job description. These young moms would pile clothes onto their carts and give me a sweet smile as they walked into the dressing room, never to be seen again for hours.

I'd chase their charming little people as they hid in the center of the round racks. The little bastards knew I couldn't reach them there. This was back in the 70s when you could threaten stranger's kids. Good times, good times.

Now and then, a mother would come out of the dressing room with some crazy outfit on, and she would ask me, "Does this look good on me?"

I'm an honest person. When I first started at Piccadilly, I would tell the truth.

"Girl, you look crazy. Now get back in the dressing room and try again."

Later, my boss would pull me aside and say, "Shelby, we are here to sell clothes, not humiliate our customers. Lie, tell the customer the outfit they picked looks great with their eyes. Whatever, Shelby, just sell, sell, sell."

My manager knew I was studying fashion, so she would have me put together outfits and staple them to the wall for displays. This worked. A lot of women would come in and point to my displays and purchase the whole outfit.

One bad dresser after another would come into Piccadilly and put together these insane outfits. I remember having nightmares of these bad dressers chasing me like zombies. I'd wake up in a cold sweat, look at the clothes in my closet, and let out a sigh of relief.

One day, a woman walked in and threw a bunch of clothes in her cart to try on. The woman came out of the dressing room with a royal blue, flowered shirt and a velvet yellow polyester polka dot skirt with fringe. I kid you not.

"How does this look? I have a really important job interview tomorrow."

Everything went into slow motion. I had already been reprimanded for telling the truth. I was on shaky ground. I turned to my manager behind the register, and she glared at me.

"Um, well, I, it, uh, the outfit really goes well with both of your eyes. I mean, both of your eyes are color coordinated, wow, uh, this outfit really champions that. I, uh, like your eyes so much." What the hell, Shelby, lying is not your strong suit.

My manager's face wrinkled up, and she went in the back to hide.

"Oh, thank you. I've always loved my eyes. Okay, ring it all up. Thank you so much."

Wow, she bought it. My manager reappeared and rang the uncoordinated woman up at the register.

Years later, I still remember standing at the front of Piccadilly, watching the uncoordinated woman jump into her Vega and speed off. She wasn't going to get that job with that crazy outfit on.

Off she goes to an unsuspecting world to make countless uncoordinated outfits; to pollute our world with her lack of color coordination. A single tear rolled down my face. You made a great sale, Shelby. Get over it.

I just attended my cousin Vinnie's wedding. He married a beautiful woman. The wedding was a black-tie affair.

The wedding was held at a country club in San Francisco. Sitting across from my husband, who looked dashing in his tuxedo, I looked down at the prettiest place settings I'd ever seen. I ran my hand over the silver-trimmed bread plate, which also had a gorgeous butter knife. I brushed my hand over the gold leaf base plates. I put the velvet napkin trimmed with white satin on my lap. Oh, Vinnie. Oh, Vinnie. You will live a joyous, color-coordinated life. I'm so happy for you. Because everyone knows color coordination is the key to a happy life.

## About The Author

Stacey is a writer, actress, stand-up comedian, producer, and voice-over talent who lives in Northern California. Her one woman show is entitled, "The Stacey Show".

"The Bus Stop", her shortfilm is available for viewing at STACEYANDRADE.YOLASITE.COM.

Look for The Stacey Show You Tube channel in 2024.

Stacey's books are available on Amazon.

Milton Keynes UK
Ingram Content Group UK Ltd.
UKHW010630040424
440620UK00001B/24